Common Terms in Computer Science

Common Terms in Computer Science

An Anthology

◆

Jesu Venedici

Writers Club Press

San Jose New York Lincoln Shanghai

Common Terms in Computer Science
An Anthology

Writers Club Press
an imprint of iUniverse, Inc.

For information address:
iUniverse, Inc.
5220 S. 16th St., Suite 200
Lincoln, NE 68512
www.iuniverse.com

Any resemblance to actual people and events is purely coincidental.
This is a work of fiction.

ISBN: 0-595-22957-3

Printed in the United States of America

Contents

◆

In the lands beyond, there stands the Thelto Canyon. It is a well-known canyon that any one person on the earth or elsewhere, especially elsewhere, knows about. It is the boundary between the two kingdoms.

There are two kingdoms that reign over the whole known land, the Kingdom of Death on our side of the Thelto Canyon, and the Kingdom of Life.

These kingdoms have been at war for the past six millennia, fighting for the total elimination of the other. We are the soldiers fighting for the advance of either realm. Who do you fight for?

PART ONE:

◆

The Program

Abstract Data Type

———————— ◆ ————————

John Miller Campbell hates Church. He despises the time he has to spend at First Baptist Church in Geyser Springs, CO, listening to some-one drone on about stupid ideas. He gets dragged there every Sunday, thrown into Sunday school classes, and forced into church services. And, he has to go every single Sunday! Every Sunday, he has to sit down on a pew for a full hour, listening to someone leading the church in singing old songs, while his parents try to force him to sing along. He never does. After the sing-along session, a short, bald, fat man steps up behind a large, fancy podium behind a short wooden table. He speaks for half an hour about irrelevant stuff, walking around in his black suit and red tie. Then, free at last! Well, almost free…

"John, your father and I are worried about you," Angela said. Angela and Fred, John's parents, were Southern Baptists who did everything any good Southern Baptist would do, proselytizing coworkers, going to church, and, unfortunately for John, dragging everyone around into church as well. They were driving home from Sunday morning service, giving John the usual 'get saved' speech.

"I know, I know. I'm a bad person that God loves so much, he's going to hate me and show no mercy until I decide that I am going to love him back. Ain't gonna happen."

"That's a horrible thing to say."

"I know. I'm sorry, Mom. I won't put down your stupid myths again."

"John, you know that's blasphemy."

"Okay. God, I know you don't exist, but I'm sorry."

"John!"

They pulled into their home, a nice wooden two-story house with red trim and a view of the mountains. John raced past the snow-covered shrubbery into the brown double doors, turned left, and raced up the spiraling staircase to the hall on the upstairs landing. He looked at the caramel colored carpet below where his parents were just walking in. Fred was about to shout up to him. Before he did, and John had to sit through another 'honor thy father and mother' speech, John turned left again and ran to the end of the hallway and into his room.

Fred and Angela Campbell walked into the middle of their sitting room, and looked at the spot were the family television set used to be, now used as a stand for religious texts, Bibles, and devotionals. They tried to maintain a family devotional, but John continuously interrupts and explains that the devotionals they read out of are just plain wrong.

John had another reason to get out of the family devotional time: the television upstairs. That was now his only connection with the normal world. Since they started going to church, John's parents had become a lot less fun. They lost the television to start devotionals, prayers, and Bible studies. The CD's the family used to listen to were now considered trash, and thrown out. John even had to throw out his music-unless he could find a way to hide it, which he did.

Once the change had occurred, John got a job. He earned enough money to buy a television set, which he could hide in his room. He started hiding stuff under his bed, and he bought a wooden chest that he could use to hide the stuff that wouldn't fit.

Now, they wanted to change his social life. Daniel Smithers was John's best friend. John liked him for his near lack of morality. John seemed to gravitate to those people, since the more popular people at

John's school were those who could behave immorally, so John stood with Daniel, taunting the little guys, stealing lunch money from fat people, and attempting to make the outcasts miserable.

Of course, all this was supposed to change with his parents' conversions. John was expected to give up not only his favorite activities and possessions, but also his friends! Well, he decided early on that God isn't good enough for him.

At school, John had always been a popular guy, and Couper High had a weird way to measure popularity: cruelty. The crueler you are to certain people, the more popular you are. John learned that he could accomplish this by staying with Daniel Smithers, whose hobby was to 'steal' from these certain people. John usually met him at the beginning of the school day, shared gossip, and went 'stealing' with him. The money they got (if any) would be shared between them. Monday, however, was a little different. John met Daniel, gave him the usual gossip, and the two started out on their rounds. The first victim was a transfer student from across the state.

David Travonette was nearly John's opposite. He grew up in church, and enjoyed it very much. So much, in fact, that he had made a profession of faith early on, and once baptized, started learning the art of proselytization. At the school he used to go to, he would spend most of his time handing out literature, and talking to anyone he could.

And John and Daniel found him doing just that. As John approached, he looked at David's green dress pants, white shirt, and red tie.

"Looks like a geek to me," he said. David turned to offer literature to his two assailants. The two started the process they had been through many a time:

"Give me your money," Daniel said as John stood ready to run in with his fist ready to give David some persuasion, but the cue never came.

"Sure. How much do you want?" David asked as the school turned to watch. Murmurs. David held out two green bills.

"Oh, by the way, I'm David. Who might ya'll be?" Murmurs and rumors filled the hallway.

Daniel stared back to a confused John.

"What the H—happened?" John asked.

"I have no idea," Daniel said,

"This never happened before. Why now? Why didn't he fight us?"

John shrugged his shoulders and walked away.

"His parents must be rich."

"No parent would give their child more than forty dollars for lunch at a school like this!"

"So why do we have forty dollars in our hands? I mean, I'm sure it was a slick trick to keep us away."

"Forty Dollars, Daniel. No way that's less than all he had. You said, 'give us your money,' so he gave us his money. All of it."

"People are to greedy to hand over everything. That's why we can still knock some people to the ground when it seems that they would know to give up."

"Well…This one gave up to fast. It's as if he didn't give up."

"What do you mean?"

"You heard the gossip goin' on about us, right? I mean, I'll bet that he handed his money over because he thought he could turn the school against us!"

"You mean he fought back—"

"In a much more effective way than anyone else thought of."

"Huh! The guy's a genius. I'll bet we could still beat him down, though. The guy's gotta have some weakness."

"Yeah. We gotta get him back. We gotta redeem ourselves."

So, they met after school and began planning. They thought about a plan to deal with him in front of the school, but then David piped up and said, "His weapon is the school. We must disconnect him from the school to win." John agreed.

"Maybe if we could give it to him privately, we could coax him into taking it publicly." They thought. They paced. They looked at each other as if to say, "This is hard," but then they looked back to say, "It will happen."

They decided to meet in an alley behind the school. The plan was to come at him the way they did before, plop him into a trashcan, and let him roll. In fact, he may even roll right out in front of the school. If so, great. They would come out and claim their victory. If not, they would keep it up until they could do it in front of the school. For now, the alley was the way to go. It was the way most people had to go home, so for those with the plans that John and Daniel had, it was perfect. The dumpster was there. Several rusted steel trashcans lined the ancient remains of an ancient lawn. All the teachers would be going to their cars on the other side of the building, and would be the way that their target would be walking. Even better, there were indentations in the building where lurkers could hide. John, who came up with the entire plan, led Daniel into the selected indentation, where they hid, watched, and waited.

"Hi. I'm David. Who are ya'll?" Daniel looked up. "It's him!"

John put his hands against the wall and prepared to jump out.

"I just can't wait!" He whispered.

"Shall we go?"

"Wait."

"Now?"

"No."

"Well?"

Some time passed as David approached.

"Now!" Both boys ran forward from their hiding spot, labels on their jeans waving like little battle flags signaling the advance of the cavalry.

They split. John ran up to face David, and Daniel took up the rear. David was surrounded as John let his meanest face show.

"Oh hi, I'm David. Who are you?" David said while he stuck out his hand.

"Your worst nightmare," came a voice from the back. David turned to see Daniel, arms raised and ready to block anything that came his way.

"Hi, Worst Nightmare, how are ya?"

"Get him!" John shouted, readying himself for anything. John threw a blow straight into David's chin. David stood still, confused. Daniel threw him a blow, and the three of them moved up the alley towards the selected trashcan, two punching and one walking in between.

Thud! David was stuffed headfirst into the trashcan, some of it's red lip rubbing off on his pants.

"Lord, help me!" He said while the can tilted and started rolling. "Lord help me to forgive..." The can started to slow down.

"Ha ha ha ha!" The school was watching the can make it's slow trip across the yard, rolling it's captive on toward...

Beeeeeeeeeeeeeep! One of the scariest sounds a person could ever hear, especially when one has rolled down a steep front yard and onto a four-lane road with no lack of traffic. Hooooooonk!

"Lord, protect..."

The faraway sound of applause while rolling down a hill would certainly make most of us bitter, especially when followed by the chorus of car horns and a symphony of cars ready to crush the can you happen to be rolling across the street in, but not David. He was used to harsh treatment from the last school. And the school before that. And before that. He had never been rolled down a hill and into the street before, but other stuff had happened, usually resulting in nothing being done. He had learned in church about the necessity of forgiveness, and he practiced more than most of us would be willing. So, when John met him in the hall the next morning, he was prepared for David to try to knock him out. So prepared, in fact, that he had a few surprises waiting with David's name on them. But, much to his disappointment, all he got was,

"Hey, your worse nightmare's associate, how are ya?" John looked back, remembering every detail of the fight they had to move David into the can. Was it a fight? John wondered. Did he even fight back? Did I ever block a single blow? I remember he gave some reluctance, but wait! Daniel was also forcing! He walked right along with us! What the H—can we do to him?

So, John met up with Daniel again, to figure out how to humiliate David.

"He doesn't seem to respond to our stunts," he explained." I think we need to find something else."

"Like what?" Daniel said, looking puzzled.

That something else came the next day, straight from David's mouth. It was a prayer. Of course, just praying didn't help John much-he had heard prayers every day of his life, and had even pretended to pray with his parents. It was what David prayed:

"Lord, I ask that you would help me to forgive those who persecute me." John suddenly realized why he hadn't been successful: he was up against someone who held to something he couldn't comprehend.

But he had an idea: Mark. Mark was a very good friend of Daniel who loved to talk. He loved to talk so much that he had the highest score in speech class that John knew of. If mark could befriend David, maybe he could talk David into fighting. If that could happen, maybe John could do something to him.

So, Friday, Mark walked up to David.

"Hi. I'm mark."

"Oh, hi, Mark, I'm David. How are you?"

"I'm cool. May I sit with you?"

"Sure."

"I've seen the way those two jerks have treated you. It's pretty rotten."

"Yeah. If only they could have I do."

"Wha?"

"If only they could have what I have."

"What's that?"

"A special relationship with my Lord."

"What the f—is that?"

"What they, and you, need."

"I feel for ya, man."

"No, I feel for you. You need a Lord."

"Why?"

"Because my Lord says…"

"I don't care about your Lord, man. Check ya later."

John was talking with Daniel as Mark walked away.

"He thinks he has some special relationship to make him better than everyone else." John stared at David, watching him pray.

"I know, Mark," he said. In his mind's eye, he could see the fat, bald preacher at First Baptist of Geyser Springs. He only wished he had listened.

Implicit Parameter

◆

David came home to the usual Wednesday evening welcome from his family: "Get to your studies so you can go to church." As it was with most of his friends, Wednesday evening was a church night. David always went, with or without parents. Most of his friends were members of the church, and most also came Wednesday evening. David always chatted with them after the service.

John went to the same church as David, but he usually found some excuse to stay home on Wednesdays so he could watch the television set he snuck into his room. Of course John was more reluctant to make excuses today, seeing how Mark had his little talk with David. Nevertheless, when the time came, so did the excuses. John stayed home yet again.

When it was time for his show to come on, the usual excitement enveloped John, but when it started, the enjoyment stopped. John could not enjoy his program, and he didn't know why. It was as if something inside of him left, and something else it had covered now stared john's brain straight in the emotional department. So, what was it?

John met up with Daniel at the usual spot the next day. As John walked up to him, he noticed that Daniel's gaze had been stolen by something. He followed it across to where David stood, holding out a piece of paper.

"He just stands there, trying to get somebody to take the paper from him." Daniel said. "I don't get it."

"I think I know what he's doing," John said as he rolled his eyes at David.

"What?"

"Has he given any out?"

"Yes, he has. Then, he got another out and started over."

"I know what he's doing." John looked away, unbelieving. He couldn't understand why someone would want to be so noticeable, yet at the same time, he wondered if David thought the same thing about him. "You know, I think I am missing out on something."

"Huh?" Daniel grunted.

"I am missing out on something. Something I need. Something that has the power to help me and heal me."

"Help you what and heal you from what?"

"I don't know. I just need to find this."

"What's this?"

"I don't know. It's something I need. Can you help me find it?"

"Talk to David. He seems to have things together."

"I know what he's got, and it's trash."

So John started on a search that many a person has made before, some successfully, others not. Like most people, he had no idea what he was looking for, or where or how to look. He just started out and hoped for the best.

English class. The teacher started a new book by Henry David Thoreau, Walden. John listened intently on this testimony of the man who had spent many years in the woods, and then wrote of his experiences. At home, John began to heed his advice. He looked through his closet for unneeded stuff. He brought the TV down to the garage, along with half his music collection. But to no avail! John felt nothing in this simplicity phase except for a burning desire to watch television and listen to the music and wear the clothes that he just threw out. This Thoreau guy didn't know so much of what he was talking about.

So, John met Daniel by the lockers again, and stated his complaints.

"I thought it would work," he said. "I can't believe that Thoreau got it wrong!"

"Talk to David. I'll bet he knows," Daniel said.

"If David knew, wouldn't I?"

"Well, I don't know. You aren't exactly into it."

"I go to church."

"Okay. You got a point."

David walked behind the two as they peaked their heads into their respective lockers.

"I'm glad I've got this," he said as he walked by.

Formal Parameter

◆

Joey Turner hates you. He hates everyone who gets in the way of his addictions. His father was a heavy drinker, spending more than the occasional long night at the bar, wasting the family's money. Of course, he did come home occasionally. But Jerry hated it when that happened, because his mother would rebuke her husband, and he would shout at her, and she at him, and a fight would break out. Whenever his parents fought, it would carry throughout the whole three-room house they lived in. Joey hates to be home. He even thought hi life would be so much better without a dad.

But that thought was soon rebuked. While he was still in the second grade, his dad's drinking started to clog his liver. The doctors tried to get him off alcohol, but he wouldn't quit. He died within the next three months.

With a deceased absentee father and a mother who works twelve hours a day, Joey had nowhere to turn. His friends at school could never understand the trouble, and the drug prevention program that the school's police officer was taking Joey's English class through didn't help either. But Joey was about to make another friend.

James Engleson was his name. He was the best friend of Jason Mitch, the friend of one of the most wanted drug dealers in Couper High. Although he was only starting to smoke at this point, Jason was being trained by to replace the dealer, should he ever be caught. He was pulling James right down the path with him, so James, naturally, introduced drinking to Joey.

James and Joey soon became dependent on alcohol, upgraded to smoking, and eventually formed a pact with Jason. They would go to Jason, buy drugs, and take them in a group, in a hopefully concealed place. Of course, drug treatment came for some, as did arrests, but they would to their drugs. It was their lifeline; Joey couldn't get over his dad's death without booze, but he never connected the booze with his dad. Instead, they just kept on boozing, smoking, and drugging themselves, as they will until death. And, two more have entered this fellowship of drugs, both having been rescued from the pit of meaninglessness and depression. Ron Veda came after the death of his mother, and Jacob Sink was looking for something fulfilling that he could do. Now, the five of them sit around a cooler of drugs and beer supplied by Jason Mitch behind the science wing of Couper High, where they stay until they can take no more (or one of them passes out, whichever comes first).

Yet today was going to be different. The Fellowship of the Beer Cooler sat around their cooler of beer and other means of salvation.

"Give me another joint," Ron said.

"I'll take another. And more beer," Joey said.

"Me too," said James.

"Alright. Whoever wants more, come forward," Mitch said. They received, paid, and started the smoking, drinking, and drugging all over again.

"And," Jacob said, "It's open ended!" They all laughed. A little too hard, as one person's laugh was heard in a classroom of the science wing, where a teacher was setting up the next day's lab. So, he or she, whoever he or she was, came out of his or her office to tell the laugher to please be quiet. But, much to his or her surprise, he or she saw that he or she was standing in front of a congregation of druggists standing around a seeming altar covered with spilt tobacco, marijuana, cocaine, and beer. But, two of the members had the good fortune to leave the service early. You see, the rusty red door stopped right by a section of shrubbery, so it formed a kind of apse. James and Joey noticed one of the walls of this apse opening, and they had screamed out, "Run," and had started running. But, the rest of the congregation only turned and saw, to their dismay, that he or she was standing there, whoever he or she was. None of them had seen him or her before, so they couldn't tell that he or she was a teacher. They had no idea of how he or she was alerted to their presence, or how he or she had found them, they only knew that they were in trouble with him or her, and that he or she was sure to alert the school to their services, and that they would be expelled after he or she took them to the office with him or her. So, she said, since he or she happened to be Mrs. Dulwimple, "This is illegal. Come with me." So, James and Joey turned to see their three other friends taken in by him or her, three downtrodden, hopeless martyrs. They had no more hope.

They next day, they were sitting in the last period class of that day, when the first serious signs of withdrawal had begun to come on.

"I miss Jason," Joey said. "I know," James said, "We need our stuff."

"I really need my stuff. I've got an empty hole to fill."

"So do I."

"Did you know that there's a liquor store that's close?"

"Really?"

"Yeah. We can go in and shoplift."

"How?"

"Ever heard of bootlegging?"

"What's that?"

"Liquor down our pants."

"Let's do it."

So, after school, the three walked into a liquor store, opened their flies, and stuffed all the liquor they could feast their eyes on down their pants. They every kind of liquor and beer you could imagine (thank

God for baggy jeans!). And, once they had filled their pants, out they went.

But, as they went out, the shop owner noticed that Joey (who had forgot to zip his fly back up) had a small portion of a whiskey bottle sticking out of his pants. So, he phoned the police, who were kind enough to wait until the two bootleggers had legged their booze to the street, but then,

"Sirens," James said. "What do we do now?" "Run," Joey exclaimed. They ran, and at first the police didn't quite realize why they were running, but Joey's fly became clear to one of the officers, so around they came and chased after the two legers.

"They're getting closer," said James, "We need to hide."

"Right," said Joey, who searched the bushes, "Right there. Follow me." And they crossed a field of yellow-green grass into some of the lushest shrubbery you could ever see. The police passed by, as the two took out their liquor. The police passed by again, and they began to drink. The police passed by yet again, and they started to pack up. "I think that should be sufficient for today. We need to save some so we don't have to rob those guys every day," Joey said.

"We can't leave. Somebody's coming this way," James said, his hands beginning to shake. Indeed, footsteps could be heard approaching, a rhythmic crunch becoming progressively louder.

"There's a hole in the back of these bushes. I bet we can get away through these," Joey said.

So, the two twisted and turned their way through the shrubs into a lush forest. Neither would admit it, but it was unfamiliar territory, but the cops had found the hideout, and they were coming through.

"Run straight this way. We should be able to find an end."

And, as Joey suggested, they ran through the trees, but no sign of an end. They kept running, and the police kept following, but Joey heard what he thought was the police stopping to turn around, so he stopped. "Hand me a cigarette," Joey said. He couldn't see any way to relieve the pressure of the moment than to sit down and have a smoke. Maybe even two. Maybe then he could think clearly and lead his friend out of the situation. But the police didn't stop, they were right behind James.

"Tired, huh?" Came a voice from behind, belonging to the officer who had recognized the liquor in Joey's pants. Joey dropped his cigarette right into a pile of dead leaves.

"Run, James, run," he said, not noticing the smoke rising at his feet. They ran one way, and the police, thinking they knew the way out, and having seen the smoke, started inching their way out of the forest, back to the shrubbery, and back to their patrol cars.

Unfortunately, neither of the two boys knew the way out of the forest and when they came up to a giant wooden wall, they were confronted with a considerable wall of flame several yards away, a wooden wall one inch from their noses, and no way to escape.

"I'm sorry, Joey, I should have never introduced you to this stuff," James shouted, his eyes beginning to tear up and shudder at the sight of the flames.

"It's okay, James. You helped me," Joey said.

"No, I didn't. Jason was using me. He needed someone to sell to so some drug dealer wouldn't be upset. I betrayed you."

"You never betrayed me. I can still trust you."

"No, you can't. You never did. You trusted chemicals." James began to put the liquor down in strategic places, a kind of shield from the harsh realities.

"No, I didn't. I trusted you. The drugs never did me any good."

"My point exactly. They never did anyone any good. They were Jason saving his hide."

The bottles exploded as the fire drew closer, and the two began to realize that they would offer no protection. They ran, but as they did so, they ran upon a wet patch of dirt. Both boys slipped into the flames from which they shall never emerge.

Real Parameter

◆

Jerry Bartolomy is one of David's new friends. He transferred in several weeks before from some Christian school in Denver. His parents wanted to keep him in some Christian schools for various reasons, so they practically starved the family to keep his tuition going.

David first saw Jerry at his church. Sunday morning, he walked over to him and shook hands.

"Hi, I'm David."

"I'm Jerry," a skinny boy said. David took a seat by him in a pew as his parents extended their hands, giving their names, Don and Mary.

"Hi. David. Pleased to meet you guys. Welcome to Geyser Springs. Good trip?"

"Yes," Don said, "It was nice. You must go to a Christian school?"

"No, I don't. In fact, I don't believe there is one around here, but I go to a school about two blocks from here."

"Is it a good school?"

"I hope so, cause it's the only one."

"Really?"

"Yep. It's not that bad. Most of the students are okay, and it's within walking distance of the church, if you live near it."

When Monday morning rolled around, David was given an address and a buddy to walk with. When they approached school, David pulled his literature out of his pockets. "A little personal evangelism," he explained, "Wanna join me?" Jerry reached out his hand to take some of the literature from David. They came and stood at the place where David always stands, and there they passed out the literature until the five-minute bell rang. "I think it's time to split and go to class," David said, "Know where to go?"

"No." Jerry hung his head.

"What room?"

"254A."

"This way."

The two made their way to a portable building, where Jerry walked in. David ran away to his class across the school. And so they remained until the next period.

The bell rang, and Jerry slowly got up and started slowly making his way through the hall to his next class, or at least what he thought was his next class, because he had no idea where to find the room. He found a door he thought would be the room and opened it. He was outside, behind the school.

"Hello, my good friend, how'd you find us?" Jason Mitch said while taking a half-burnt joint out of his mouth. "So, tell me, what do you want?"

"Nothing," Jerry said.

"Come on, man, you've gotta need something, you can't just walk out here, now what is it?"

"Nothing. I came out here because I can't find my next class."

"Try some beer. It's really, really good, and just what a new guy like you needs to relieve the stress of school."

"No. I need to find my class."

"Try it. You need it."

"No, I don't. I'm looking for roo—"

"We don't care. Just join our group…who the h—are you?" Jason asked, red faced. Jerry looked behind him. David came leading what appeared to be an administrator into the hall. Jerry ran into the school. Jason ran away. David stared.

"How'd you find them," he asked, "No one's been able to find them in the three years they've been here."

"I can't find my class," Jerry said.

"Dang, you must be from a really small school." David looked at his schedule. "This way."

The rest of the day passed relatively eventless, no more lucky saves by David, that is, and it came time for David to walk Jerry home.

"Who was that guy this morning?" Jerry asked.

"That was a druggie," David said, "The administration knew for a long time that there's been one on campus, but I think you've helped them find the actual location, but I think that he'll change it on them."

"Druggie?"

"Yeah. Someone on drugs. Weird guy."

"Why?"

"Never saw it at your school?"

"I guess not."

"Some people think that drugs will help them, give them a better life."

"Why?"

"I don't know. They just think that. Don't worry about those two. Once they see you with me, they oughtta leave you alone."

"Why?"

"I had an ugly run-in with them, too. I started witnessing, and they started running."

"Why?"

"I've never been able to figure it out, but they're afraid of me. Don't worry about it. If they try to pull anything, witness."

"Right."

"I guess this is where you get off." David was now standing in front of an old building that seemed so old, he wondered why it isn't condemned. He watched as Jerry walked inside, and he wondered how his parents could have afforded a Christian school.

Time passed for some time until it happened again:

"Hey, man, you cool," someone said behind Jerry. He turned. Jason Mitch was sitting with four others around a cooler. "Join the fun."

"Who are you?" Jerry asked.

"I'm Jason. This is Ron, Jacob, James and Joey." As he said their names, each of them waved. "Everyone, this is our special new friend, what's your name?"

"Jerry."

"Jerry. Join the fun, Jerry."

"No, thank you."

"Come on, man, you know you need the help."

"What?"

"Come on, man. I've seen the little shack you call home. No way you can enjoy it."

"Actua—"

"So put some pizzazz into your life. Have a beer."

"Actually, I don't need anything from you."

"Sure you do. Come on, man, don't deny yourself the extra sustenance you need."

"Which I received after making my profession of faith."

"What?"

"I don't need your stuff because I've got God's stu—"

"Get the h—away from me!"

And Jerry never had to worry about the druggies again. Now, the two sat on the couch in the Travonette's den, Bibles open on the floor beside tables littered with homework, as would happen in their study sessions. They would work until one had a verse to read, then the Bibles would be picked up, read, and gently laid beside the table until someone wanted to read from one again. In the mean time, David and Jerry would be working on the night's subject.

David's mother came up.

"Do either of you know Joey Turner or James Engleson?" She asked. Her head was bobbing side to side in the manner that it always does when some bad news hits home.

"No. Never heard of 'em," David said.

"Well, I heard that they died today."

"Really?"

"Yes. They died in a forest fire started by their cigarettes. The newscaster said that the blaze came on them suddenly after some stolen bottles of liquor had exploded nearby."

"That's horrible," David said.

"I think I might have met them," Jerry said as his head bobbed downward. "I had another run-in with the group, and I think there might have been a Joey and a James."

"Glad you know Him?"

"Oh, yes. Amen."

Then David and his family, heads bowed, whispered to each other, "Amen."

Class

---◆---

Friday Morning, John walked up to a nervously pacing Daniel.

"Hey, guy, what up?" He asked. Daniel looked over to David, who had given out another paper, and started his pacing again.

"Why in f—ing h—do they have to do that?"

"I thought we've been through this, man, they're weirdoes. They only do that to make the church grow."

"They've been at it to much. Too hard. Someone wanted to hit them today."

"So?"

"Someone tried to. John, there's no way someone would take a beating by one of the fattest football players on campus just to make the church grow, now would they?"

"You need to see my parents. You don't know how hard core some of these people can be."

"It doesn't make sense, John. He's too different, too religious, too…something. It doesn't make sense. He should have stopped by now."

"Why?"

"Puntz?"

"You mean?"

"He really did threaten them. In fact, isn't that him?"

A fat senior walked up, raised his fist, and shouted, "I thought I told you to get out!"

"Hi! How are you," David started. The other guy just stared down at them.

"SHUTUP!" He ran up to them, arms waving. John shut his eyes. David stood, holding Jerry's hand as Jerry trembled and they prayed.

SLAAAAAAAAAAMMMMMMMMM. The two of them were sent flying for several yards into the red brick wall behind them. Puntz walked away, and David helped a trembling Jerry walk back to the spot, where they discarded the wrinkled tract and pulled a fresh one. Daniel stared at John in disbelief.

"You want to tell me that that's just pure religion? It can't be. You have to be wrong, John. You just gotta be."

John stared at the two across the hall.

"What happened?"

"Puntz threw them against the wall, and they just walked back."

"That must have been ten yards!"

"They walked back. The little guy's trembling, but David looks like nothing happened. Why, John, Why?"

"I just don't get it."

John and Daniel stared at the two scraped evangelists standing across the hall as Puntz came by them again. Pow, Jerry was down again, but he was soon standing by David again. He put his hand up to his jaw, and both hand and jaw were soon deep crimson with blood. Daniel's face turned red. "That really takes some guts."

John started walking away. Daniel followed. As they walked into the locker room, Daniel kept reliving the scene he had just emerged form.

"Why, John, why. I'll bet the little guy's still standing there, bloody jaw and all."

"Trust me, Daniel, there's nothing special to it."

"I just need to find out."

So, Sunday morning, John had a special surprise: Daniel had come to church.

"Daniel, what the H—," John said as he watched his friend pass by to a pew near the front. Of course, Fred turned around and frowned at John. "Hey, Daniel, wait for me!" John yelled as he ran away from his pew barely in time to escape his dad's angry grasp.

"Daniel, what are you doing here?" John asked as he came into his pew.

"I told you John, I need to see why those two are passing that stuff out." John slumped in his seat, trying to get as low as possible. Fred walked by, looking intently at every pew. "John, what is it?" Daniel asked.

"Shutup and lean over. Parents." John whispered into his ear. Daniel leaned over.

"The bald guy?"

"Yep, that's him. Be quiet. Act like I'm not here."

"He's gone."

"Good."

They sat through that service together. Somewhere towards the end, the preacher gave an altar call.

"All have sinned and fall short of the glory of God," the preacher read. Daniel was a bit confused. What's sin, he wondered, have I done any?

John, who had slept through most of the service, began to wake up.

"Hey John, what's sin?" Daniel asked as John started to look back, not noticing the preacher was still on the pulpit.

"What?" John looked forward to see the preacher's eyes locked onto his.

"The wages of sin is death," the preacher said.

"What's sin?" Daniel asked again.

"I have no idea. I think it's some thing you do, but I'm not sure what. If someone tries to talk to me about it, I just pretend that I'm uncomfortable with the idea. It keeps the pastor away, and that's how I suggest you react to him when he starts talking to you about it." John said.

"I think I'd rather like to hear him out. I'm curious."

"You'll be sorry."

"How do you know?"

"I know, Daniel. I've fell victim to nearly everybody's efforts to convert me. You won't like it. They don't make sense, and they don't leave you alone."

"You just don't listen."

"Yeah, well, I've been around these guys. I know the message. I may not know the terms, but I can give you the message without the hassle."

"Okay, shoot. Never mind."

The church got up. Another song was sung, and afterwards, John talked to Daniel.

Monday morning was another meeting with the evangelists and Puntz. Daniel was, again, nervously pacing.

"Hey, Daniel. What's up?" John started as he walked towards him.

"They're at it again." Daniel said, pointing to Puntz as he walked up to his favorite set of victims. "How can they take it?"

"I don't know, but I'm sure that the respect that they get from the members of their church must really help."

"He threw them against the wall. He's not leaving."

"They'll give up. They just need some persuasion."

"He did it again. He's just standing and waiting. David's holding something up."

"They're trying to evangelize their troubles away."

"It's not working. Puntz threw them again. He's getting really frustrated."

"They'll stop. Everyone has limits."

"I don't expect them to."

"I do. Even the most religious member of my church can't hold out against that forever."

"You're right. They've got to stop eventually."

The bell rang, and David split from his partner. Puntz shouted after them,

"What I thought!"

"Five minutes to classes," John observed.

"That's why they split," Daniel asked.

They stared at each other until they realized that they, too, would have to leave. Daniel's mind came back to the day before. I wonder what sin is, he wondered, John doesn't seem to know; yet it is something commonplace according to John's preacher. 'Wages of sin is death.' What does that mean? Death comes for sinners? It comes for everybody, yet John tells me that some can pray to escape this. What is this death? Well, what's sin? John knows it's bad, so I guess some bad thing. 'All have sinned.' I guess that means that I have sinned, too. What have I done? I need to speak with that preacher.

Daniel began planning a way to get a hold of the preacher when an administrator came on the loudspeaker:

"Attention all students, we express consolation to the friends and family of Joey Turner and James Engleson. The school administration would like to take a moment of silence in honor of these students."

Suddenly, Daniel understood, "The wages of sin is death." Well, at least he thought he understood.

PART TWO:

———— ◆ ————

The Central Processing Unit

Recursion

◆

Jerry was not always so fulfilled. In fact he had a very trying time as soon as he started out at Bush Middle School in Denver. He hardly knew anyone as a friend. Unfortunately, he did know some people, and more than a few, who seemed to believe that it was their duty to let Jerry know about not only his loneliness, but also every other fault they perceive Jerry to have.

As Jerry started out, he didn't have to many problems, but it was when people started to get to know him that the problems started. His dad worked at the local fish cannery for minimum wage for twelve hours a day, and his mother hardly knew how to be sympathetic to company. One thing Jerry never understood is that it was considered "bad" to have a parent working in the fish industry, which Jerry didn't learn until it was to late, and when he did, his mother didn't know how to be sympathetic enough to sense when Jerry's had a bad day, if he ever had a good day.

So, Jerry would come home angry, hurting, and abandoned, yet his mother had no clue, so Jerry would be almost immediately ordered out into the backyard to do some kind of odd job, and not only that, but told in a most rude tone.

Far, far away into the universe is another house, but a house of a different kind. It is the house of a thing called Melech Ha-Olam. Melech Ha-Olam is a very kindly old soul, very concerned about the proceedings on the earth; very interested in some claim he had once had on the inhabitants down below. But he spends all his time sitting in front of a cliff, crying.

Jerry had to get up again, as morning had come, and he was feeling not at all excited about it, as he could see no reason to get up, so he just lay there. His mother tried pulling the covers away, but he still lay there until his mother pulled the bottom sheet out from under him, and he started to very slowly arise like a wounded deer. His mother watched him and said, "Oh, you slowpoke, move it." She meant it jokingly, but it didn't exactly come out that way, but it came out in a considerably angrier voice, as it does every morning, five days a week. Jerry ate his breakfast, dressed, and arrived at school to the usual cheers of his peers, who had no reluctance to tell him how repulsive it is to have a dad who works at a fish cannery, and it was with this noise that he found his room, where his classmates continued to tell him how much they hate his being in class. So it continued for several weeks before someone planted a thought in his head.

The person was someone who had never gotten to know anyone very closely, but he had had a particularly bad day. When he saw Jerry, he walked to him and, probably to let off some steam, said to him, "Why don't you do us all a favor. Go off and die somewhere." Jerry took this idea and smiled. That's what I'll do, he thought, I'll go off and die somewhere. Far off in his palace, Melech Ha-Olam started mourning again.

Jerry had no idea how to pull off his new reason for living, but he was sure glad the idea came to him. He tried to go the easiest route possible: the family gun. His dad had spent some time in the local police force, before he decided that it was a boring job, and went to the cannery. It put Jerry's mother in a pretty sour mood, but it did give the family a handgun that would never be used again, unless…

Jerry went through his dad's underwear drawer until he found the old gun. He stuck it in his trousers and took it with him into his room. Once there, he opened the revolver as he had seen his dad do many times before to see if it was loaded, but fortunately for him, and unfortunately for his plans, it wasn't. His dad must have kept the ammunition somewhere in the house, but he would have to search later. He would have to go to school again.

The next morning, he got up with some inspiration, which melted as soon as he got inside the door. As he went home, he thought about the many times he had seen his father unload the gun. There was a place he always put the bullets, but where? He could remember his dad opening the revolver, it's black arm and silver cartridge, and he could remember the silver capsules being taken out one by one and carefully put somewhere. The jewelry box! That's it! Jerry could remember his mother getting somewhat upset about finding her necklaces mixed with expired ammo. Maybe the live ammo was there, too. Jerry checked when he got home, and it was.

His mother went through her usual chore routine, and Jerry figured he might as well wait to load the revolver. After all, his mother might appreciate one last chore session. Melech Ha-Olam started mourning again.

That night, he got permission to go for a walk, one that he intended to never return from. He had the revolver concealed in his pants pocket as he went out the door for the playground where he had seen most of his school buddies during his earlier years. Tearing up, he began to remember those earlier, happier years. Then, his mind wandering to more recent years, Jerry loaded the revolver and brought it to his head.

Melech ha-Olam was staring off the edge of a cliff to another cliff with no apparent bottom to a figure with a gun to his head. He was desperately trying to pull the gun down, trying to keep this figure from the horrors that would meet it at the bottom of the cliff, and when he realized that he could not reach the figure, he wept bitterly...

Encryption

———————— ◆ ————————

Once, the two cliffs had been one giant land that Melech Ha-Olam shared with some very close friends, Manny and Evette. They had a very strong friendship. Melech Ha-Olam would come over to be with his two friends every morning, and the times they would have were very happy and special to both parties. Manny and Evette would usually get some new trinket that caught their attention, and Melech Ha-Olam would get to spend more time with his favorite friends. They loved each other very much, and Melech Ha-Olam more so.

But as time went on, and the three shared the majesty of Melech Ha-Olam's palace, a rebel came around the neighborhood. This man, Lucis, was a hated enemy of Melech Ha-Olam, and believed that he was just as good as Melech Ha-Olam, and one day, he had a notion to rob somebody. Possibly because he was the richest one in the neighborhood, but more likely because he wanted to prove to the whole world that he is better than Melech Ha-Olam, he decided to try to take Melech Ha-Olam's most precious belonging from him.

Just one problem, though. Melech Ha-Olam didn't seem to have a prized possession, as he would gladly give anything he could to Manny or Evette. So, maybe, just maybe, Lucis could make these friends of Melech Ha-Olam turn on their best friend. So, as Manny was taking a walk with Evette, the villain came up to them and tried to fill their hearts with hatred. As he was sneaking up behind them, he tried to listen in for a good starting point. He got one when Manny said, "My, isn't Melech Ha-Olam a good friend?" The question was usually staged to let Evette talk about the latest trinket that had been given to her by the gracious guest. This time, however, Lucis came up with his starting line:

"What the h—are you talking about? Melech Ha-Olam? a good host? That snob is so…so…he's so rude! He took a bunch of trinkets from me, and now that I came back to claim them, he claims he doesn't have them. I'll bet he decided to give them away. It would be just like him. I'll bet you have my stuff."

"What kind of stuff did you have?"

"Well, for starters, I had a mink coat that I intended to give my girlfriend."

"He gave you a mink coat just a few days ago."

"Yes, and a silver ring."

"Which you got yesterday."

"A gold necklace?"

"Yeah."

"Three hens in an evergreen basket?"

"I got that today! Ooh, that makes me so mad!"

"What about a chainsaw?"

"He gave me one a year ago to help clear some shrubbery to build a house."

"The guy is so ornery! I can't believe he decided to just give out everything that meant anything to me! I'll also have you know my girl-friend left me because of that stuff."

"Can we help?"

Those words are just what Lucis wanted to hear. He never really owned those items that he claimed to own; he only knew those things because he had been through the couple's house the night before. But he knew that he had them right where he wanted them—ready to shape their heads and fill it with more un-loyal thoughts.

The two came to breakfast with their good friend in question, Melech Ha-Olam, when he produced another of his trinkets. This time, as had never happened before, Manny was quick to decline. Melech Ha-Olam seemed a bit alarmed, but he took the declination fairly lightly, and said,

"Well, okay, I think it could actually look very nice on my mantle in the den." Manny was disgusted at this suggestion, but held it in. After breakfast, the two were visited again by the villain, Lucis, who immediately asked them, as he had been through Melech Ha-Olam's grocery list, "You haven't by any chance a mina bird, have you?"

"Well, Melech Ha-Olam had one that he tried to rub off on us. I think he decided to put it on his mantle in his den."

"What does it look like?"

"It is a rather small bird, about six inches in length, two inches high. It is black with orange stripes, and it has a red head."

"Yep. That same bird was stolen from the mantle in my sitting-room just yesterday."

"Well, we could take a message into him that you want it back."

"I don't think it would work very well, cause, you see, I came over yesterday after my chat with you two, and requested that he return my chainsaw so that I can chop some firewood for my family back home, where it shall get very cold soon."

"You can take mine."

"That would be the appropriate thing to do, since your chainsaw happens to be mine."

"Oh, I see."

"Anyway, I don't think that your friend will be very quick to give up the mina bird. I think it will simply have to be stolen back."

"Wait a minute! Don't think that I'll try to take that mina bird. If you really need it, I'm sure you can deal with it yourself."

"I have no reason to be inside Melech Ha-Olam's palace, yet you do, since you have breakfast every morning with him, if I am not mistaken."

"Okay. I'll see what I can do."

"Thank you."

Manny discussed the matter with his wife, so that they would know what to do the next morning. When they got to breakfast, however, Melech Ha-Olam seemed very troubled about something, and the first thing beside the greeting that came out of his mouth was,

"I must warn you, A villain has been around here trying to rob from me, and I believe that he is trying to pull you away from my friendship and protection. If you try to rob me of anything, consequences will have to result, and I am afraid that it will be very catastrophic."

Manny had had enough. He became very red in the face when he heard Melech Ha-Olam say this. He simply got up and almost screamed out of his frustration,

"Okay, thief, I think It's time to give all the stuff back that you stole."

"Oh dear, I se he has gotten to you. I assure you that I took nothing. Lucis is the thief. He has no wish but to take everything that is of value away, and since you are the only thing of value that I own, he is trying to steal you."

"How can you steal a person?"

"He's very close, actually."

"You steal things, not people."

"I am afraid you are mistaken."

"Oh, shut up."

They ate breakfast in silence that morning, Lucis standing outside the window celebrating his new victory, and the three inside the palace dining room eating in silence. Then, Manny started whispering to Evette. Melech Ha-Olam suddenly looked up, an expression of shear dread on his face.

"Please don't go down this road. You don't know what lies down the path."

"No, actually, you don't know what lies down the path of not taking other people's things." And he continued to whisper.

Evette started inching toward Melech Ha-Olam as Manny waited for the opportunity to sneak off to the den. It came, and he was off. Lucis started jumping around outside so much, you would have believed him to be a lunatic had you seen him.

Several minutes later, they were all moved to a place in the middle of nowhere. Evette asked, "What's happening?" Melech Ha-Olam took back his mina bird with a painfully grieved expression on his face.

"You have given yourselves over to lucis. You are no longer worthy to be around."

The ground began to break, and soon the two groups were separated, Melech Ha-Olam staring longingly across at Manny's offspring, and Manny's offspring staring back across this infinite canyon. Lucis now owns the entire human race.

Abstraction

◆

Joey Turner and James Engleson started once they saw their surroundings. They were in what appeared to be a large holding cell. They couldn't remember how they got there, or what they were doing; all they knew was that they didn't want to be here. They looked at each other, both seeming unmarked and in good keeping, no sign of the fire that they had been in while they were still on the earth, of which they had no memory. They just sat and stared at the door, and at each other.

"Hey, Joey, think the door's locked?" James asked.

"I don't know. I'll bet it is. Anyway, I think I'd rather have a smoke first." He reached into his pocket to find his cigarettes, only to find that he had neither cigarettes nor even pockets.

"James, do you have any smokes?"

"I think so, in my…" James tried to find his pockets, only to find that he had none. The two were dressed in some kind of a black robe that seemed very uncomfortable and hot.

"I hope I shan't be in here much longer, I'll go through withdrawal if I don't get my stuff soon."

"James, we both have that problem, but I'm afraid that we'll be in here for a while."

"Try the door."

Joey got up and walked to the door, but his step became slow, unsure, and almost dreadful.

"I'm sure that there's nothing bad on the other side, but I can't try. I'm too scared." At that, both boys began to tremble.

"I think I can recall something about a fire," James said.

"I think we may have seen one recently," Joey agreed.

"A fire, oh yeah, and a forest."

"A fire and a forest. James, you are very creative."

"I don't know, man, this idea of mine seems very real."

"A forest fire, right?"

"I think so."

"I don't think I want to hear this."

"I think I'm going to try the door." At that, both of them started trembling again, as James walked to the door, slowly and with deliberation as if he was fighting himself every step of the way. He reached the door and tried the knob. It turned, but the door was stuck.

"Oh, man," he murmured, "I really want out." But deep down, both boys were really somehow relieved to find the door stuck. Suddenly, James stood up as if something had been given to his mind.

"Jason Mitch!" He yelled.

"I wonder what happened to him."

"I think he was expelled. But whatever the case, He's walking outside our room."

"Really?"

"Yeah. You know what else, Joey? We're dead."

"Doesn't seem that way."

"Remember the fire? We died in it. The liquor bottles exploded, and I ran, and fell face down in the mud. As I looked up, I saw fire above me, and beside me, and in front of me, and behind me. It felt like the middle of July in Dallas, only worse."

"You've been to Dallas?"

"Yeah. Summer vacation. Texas weather is hot."

"I think we may be about to experience something a little hotter. The door is opening, James."

A large being with a strange semblance of a person opened the door and stood in the boys' cell with them. Each could feel a very profound affection for them on the part of this 'it,' whatever it was, but it's very presence made them wish that they were in the worst torture chamber of a Nazi prison camp rather than where they were now.

"I see that my new arrivals are awake and ready for judgment, hm?" The thing said.

"Please, no!" James blurted, but he knew he could get no reprieve. Both boys had started trembling again at the mention of the word 'judgment,' and as they walked about the palace, they could hardly stand because of some kind of fear or nervousness that seemed normal but still very weird. "I was right. What now?" James asked under his breath as they were brought to a line of people in shaking black robes.

"Don't worry, James, God is supposed to be a merciful God. If that's true, he won't send us to Hell, but if that notion's as false as it seems right now, try to sell yourself with all the good that you've done. Surly that can buy our salvation."

But, unfortunately for the old best friends of the Fellowship of the Beer Cooler, the judgment process was a very simple one. They saw Jason standing in front of the biggest white throne you could imagine, and he seemed as if he was about to speak, but couldn't. Judgment was passed on most of the black robes without any dissent from the defendants, but the occasional complaint was ended very quickly with a statement by the thing on the throne, and the trembling black robe wearer nodded, and slipped past a door that seemed to lead to a sudden cliff.

Then it was time for Joey to come before the throne. A book was opened and searched. Several other books were opened when the throne's inhabitant didn't find whatever it was looking for. It began looking at the several humongous volumes that lay open before him, and then found what it was looking for.

"Turner, Joey. Hated his father, dishonored both his parents. Became addicted to alcohol in spite of a promise made to his mother that he would not drink. Became drunk on several occasions, and even lead another into drinking with him." The thing on the throne went on for days, listing in detail every thing that Joey had ever done, or thought. Joey began to tremble harder as he realized the great accumulation of evil he had performed over his life. He tried to weasel his way out of what he knew would come:

"But you see, sir, I also did a great deal of good in my life. I volunteered for several charities on several occasions, helping with fundraisers that helped feed people and possibly saved a great number of lives."

"So what," the thing on the throne said, "It doesn't make a difference. While it is true that you helped people, you lived in iniquity. I can't let that come in and defile my palace." James walked up to try to defend his friend.

"You say that you love people, right?"

"Yes," the throne thing said.

"Why do you think it's loving to send people into that pit over there?" The throne thing turned to face James, and then decided to take a little different approach. He opened the first book that he had opened with Joey, and searched for a long time. Then he started searching in his other books, and said,

"Engleson, James. Helped a drug dealer's friend to gain territory by betraying a friend to drugs, and introducing two others, one of whom he pretended to be friends with, while only trying to keep him in a drug circle, and not to mention, helped the same person die in that fire, and inspired that person to rob that store you did before you came here in that fire that you two started. Need I go further?"

"No! Please, no."

"Well, since it is the usual judgment protocol, I think I will…" The thing on the throne went on for hours, stating every single deed ever performed by the two and by each one of them solo. "Do either of you know who I am?" It asked when it had finished.

"God?" Both boys said in unison, hoping that this profession would help get them out of the terrible predicament that faced them.

"Right. I am Melech Ha-Olam, and I can still remember when I put your ancestors together, and we had a nice, quiet little life on this side of the canyon, but Manny, your ancestor, decided to let a thief talk him into stealing from me. As soon as he put his hands on the object he wanted, it was over." Tears were flowing freely from the throne thing's eyes. "I love you all, I loved him, and her, but I can't have corruption on this side of the canyon. It would undo me. I know you were hoping that you just bought yourself a reprieve, but I'm sorry. You are condemned."

The two were quiet, and even though both were ready to speak out, they couldn't. Both realized that the punishment was just, and they turned to face the door that had been opened. Full of dread, they put one foot in front of the other until they were out the door and fell into a lake of fire between the two canyon walls

Inheritance

---◆---

David was out for a walk one afternoon several years ago, while he was trying to pray about some trouble he had been having at school. God didn't seem to be hearing, even though the religious leaders told him that God would hear anything, but then again, God hasn't really done anything in the world. Where is God?

"God is everywhere," the religious leaders like to tell him. Well, he can't but be inspired by that thought, but then he looks around him and prays,

"God, show yourself. If you can hear me, let me know. I need your help. I need you." God never shows.

And back to the religious leaders he goes, who tell him to just pray and believe. He does.

"God, I need help." It never comes. Where is God?

Some people have tried to answer that question. They can be seen in the town square, fasting and doing their respective ascetic practices, as they have been doing for hundreds of years, and still they stand, sit, fast, nibble at their hands, whip themselves, inflict other types of pain to themselves that is unimaginable to you and me, and with them is the heart's cry of nearly every man, woman, and child on the planet, and now David joined the cry. People died in the Middle East who had never seen a bit of food. Wars were fought in the name of racial cleansing, some new god that sprang up out of someone's desperate heart, and justice. Even in the United States, where the unrest in the rest of the world seems to be at a stand still, two skyscrapers have been toppled by one of those mid-eastern religious weirdoes. Kids have taken guns into their classes and shot their classmates.

David ran up to the local temple again. He was getting desperate enough to bring the family pet in to sacrifice. He was even ready to join forces with the local shamans. The world had too many uncertainties, and David was getting more and more scared as time went on. Thoughts flooded his head, such as, what if my school sees the next massacre? What If I die in that? Of course, someone would do something to put David into a worst frame of mind. And he would usually respond by praying one of his prayers, but why? Prayer never worked, never in David's life had he seen an answered prayer.

The news ran another story about a gun found in someone's locker. This time, it was at Geyer Middle School, David's school! He couldn't believe it, but then again, he could. The reality began to hit him again.

As he lay down to try to sleep again that night, he again began to dream of a God, a being in a palace across a very deep canyon. He only wished he could find the way across that canyon, but if the palace was there, what was there to stop him? He wondered if there was any way to cross the canyon, but then he wondered how to find this canyon. Still, he believed that in some far-away place, there was a real canyon, with a real God, and maybe just the same God that could give the answers to David's fears, and even heal the world of it's problems. Still, God lay on the other side of the canyon, wherever it was.

As David woke up the next morning, the image came back to him of this canyon that he had dreamed of the night before. He was sure that plenty of people were trying to cross the canyon, but why wasn't it working? What if those people need something they don't have. He came to school again, and came home, and studied, and went to bed. And dreamed again.

As he dreamed, he saw the people standing by the canyon, who were trying to cross, but they had no equipment. They looked down, and they saw a lake of fire where they knew that anyone who had to cross this canyon in a hurry would end up. They were literally stuck on the side, waiting for something that would never come. Every person was trying to build a bridge, a rope, or some other method of crossing, but whenever someone would be close to long enough, the equipment would break and everyone would have to start over again. No one had managed to make it all the way across yet.

Of course, there were the ones who thought they would be able to find the way across when they have to, who just jumped over the edge and fell in with the rest of the poor deceased in the lake of fire.

So, where would the equipment come from? David could not think of anything that anyone had that would be able to get any one person across this canyon successfully. As he saw these perplexed people standing on the side of the canyon, he heard the words ringing through his head, "You are not worthy to be here. I cannot allow corruption into my palace."

He couldn't understand, but he knew that the religious people of his day wouldn't either. But the voice explained, "The reason that your people aren't getting across is that you have corrupted yourselves. Otherwise every one of you would be across."

Then, another entered. He was the king of this entire world, King Lucis. He stared David in the face and said, "You belong to me, and you always will. Don't you forget that."

Constructor

◆

Melech Ha-Olam looked over the side of the canyon to see what was happening on the other side, and he was utterly shocked, horrified, and devastated. He was watching as a schoolboy held a gun up to another. He was, needless to say, so shocked, that he started shouting, reaching, and groping. He became so wild, in fact, that he scared most of his servants, but as they ran away, he became even wilder. "No! Put it down!" He shouted over the canyon as he tried to reach across the canyon to grab the weapon, and even tried jumping across, but to no avail. The boy across the canyon was able to go through with his plans. He stuck another, smaller gun up to his head, and the process started all over again. Melech Ha-Olam began wildly shouting, groping, and jumping, trying to stop the figure from meeting the demise that would come to it at the bottom of the canyon, but to no avail. Melech Ha-Olam wept bitterly.

And then, our good friend Jerry came into vision. Of course, Melech Ha-Olam had tried to get through to Jerry, to communicate his love and his strength, but the canyon was still too wide. There Jerry stood, unreached, ready to go into the lake of fire below. Melech Ha-Olam started trying to yell to him, to comfort him, to something him, but nothing he could say could get through. He went inside and tried to think. He was staring across to a world that was in desperate need of something, and he had to get across. But how could that happen?

PART THREE:

———◆———

The Compiler

Iteration

---◆---

Standing on the side of the canyon, there are three men. Well, there actually considerably more than three men, but there are three men that have done the most work in the crossing attempts. Their names are, Ron, Tony, and Karol.

Ron is a good guy. He does his best to act right all the time, and he's never done any really bad, bad stuff. He has had some minor slips, but nothing that not everyone on the earth has done. So, if anyone can get across the canyon, Ron can, because he is the most righteous man on the earth.

As he lives his daily life, and allows his righteousness to show through, he can be righteous enough to put another inch on a bridge that stands on the side of the canyon. And, once the bridge is long enough, he can put it over the side and try to cross. And, hopefully, once he can try to cross, he can become the first human being ever to cross the canyon successfully.

Today, he was very excited when he got up because, as he looked over from his tent at the very edge of camp, he could see that the bridge he was making was long enough to half-way cross the canyon. He had only been working for the last twenty years, so maybe he would have enough righteousness collected to cross over the canyon before he dies. Anyway, it's good news, considering no one has ever had enough to even make it halfway across.

So, he started out on another day's work, making plans to spend his retirement, and all of eternity, on the other side of the canyon. When someone started to shout at him, he would simply be patient with that person, and try to remain calm. He tried to forgive every one of those people who would cause him harm, and even invited some of them over to camp for dinner. Every time he had an occasion, righteousness shone through, and another inch could be added to his bridge.

And every morning, he would grow a day older, but his bridge would grow considerably longer. One morning, he looked out to check the length, and he became very excited. He ran out to measure the bridge. It was long enough! All the dreams he had of retiring from his job came crawling back from years ago, when he looked out to see that his bridge was halfway there. He ran into the camp and back out, and started jumping and shouting. Other camp members walked out and asked, "What's the noise," and he just pointed out to his bridge and yelled out, "I can make it!"

The whole camp came out once they heard this shout. All of the camp members wanted to be first to cross.

"Wait a minute," Ron said, "I've worked hard for this. I'm not about to let forty years of righteousness go to waste, but I'll let one other person come with me."

"All right," the camp head said, "You go first, and Jerry, you can go after.

The camp watched as Ron and Jerry positioned the bridge to be pushed across the canyon. It didn't make it. They couldn't muster the strength to keep it from dipping into the burning fire below.

"Crap. Ten more years of righteousness," Ron said, "Well, I guess I might as well get back to being good. Crap."

Ten years later, the bridge was long enough again. The camp knew that, even though only Ron and Jerry would get to go out, the whole camp would have to take part in the positioning of the bridge. They built a very large wench and waited for about a week, working to make sure that the bridge never hit the bottom of the canyon. Finally, they built an anchor to hold the end of the bridge when it came to position, and it did, and the bridge rose up and jammed itself to the other side.

`"Hurray!" The camp shouted. It was time for the explorers to go. Slowly, side-by-side, they walked to the bridge's landing. Ron started first, and slowly he walked out to the bridge made of his own righteousness, which, unfortunately, could not support Jerry, who stepped out and fell through the bottom.

But, Ron kept on walking across on this bridge of righteousness, but one little problem. It wasn't pure. There were certain impurities from times that he shouted at an old lady in anger, and other downfalls. These impurities weakened the bridge, so as Ron walked on, the righteousness it was made out of became less and less pure until he was standing over nothing but pure unworthiness. So, right in the middle of the canyon, Ron, too, fell to burn forever in that great lake of fire sitting in the middle of the canyon, spanning from wall to wall. And there, he and Jerry simply stare at each other and cry out in pain.

Infinite loop

———————— ◆ ————————

Tony was standing beside his tent as he watched Ron's fall. As he watched this great man drop straight into oblivion, he realized that he was next. He already had his own bridge going, only instead of Ron's righteousness, Tony was making his bridge from pure good works. Good old good works, never become un-pure, or at least we hope not. Like Ron, Tony now had a bridge that was half way long enough, except that Tony could make his a little faster.

He made his bridge by doing a good work, and attaching it to the rest of the frame. It had taken about fifteen years for Tony to get to this point. Now, he decided to start speeding things up so he could get across a bit faster. Like Ron, Tony had this marvelous dream of the other side of the canyon, where he would never volunteer, help an old lady cross the street, or even help a needy friend again. He would sit in his little beach house and watch the waves ripple on shore. But he had a canyon to cross first.

So, he started work right away. He decided to go to public schools to tutor kids. He helped many a child learn his basics, and doubtless changed many a life. Many a person will earn more money than they could have hoped to previously, thanks to Tony.

And he helped libraries get their books straight. He helped libraries arrange shelves, reshelf, and even make shelves. He moved probably over a thousand tons of books during his time, arranging, rearranging, and loading and unloading for transfers. Not only that, but he worked without break, beside a fifteen-minute break period for his lunch. After which he would get back to work until six O'clock. The libraries loved Tony.

And, as time went on, and the bridge became longer, he decided that he was going to avoid a mistake that Ron made: He was going to build supports for his bridge. So, when he got home that night, he started taking stuff off his bridge to use as supports. Then, he made a landing and fastened his bridge to the side, and started rebuilding the bridge, section by section, including a considerable number of supports. It was a good idea, only the bridge would still be corrupted by any bad works that he's done. So, sometimes, a support would weaken and fall off, some times a part of the bridge would fall. And Tony would have to work to replace it.

Tony started working for the charities, packaging, distributing, and serving food for homeless people at more soup kitchens than an army could count on all their appendages combined. He got into sorting and distributing clothing, books, toys, and food simultaneously. And while he was doing this, he still came home and built a full-scale arch-support bridge with his works. And as he worked, his bad works would always come in and corrupt the bridge. One day, he was out over the middle of the canyon when the structure became too weak. Several supports had become so corrupted that they fell out, and enough support had fallen that a section of the bridge fell. This left Tony out to hang on a huge chunk of corrupt good works, tilting slowly over. As he started to work his way back to the side, the bridge began to fall more rapidly, and Tony never made it back to camp. He sits with Ron and Jerry, crying out with pain.

Logical Error

◆

Ron and Tony were gone, and this left Karol to do his work. His work, fortunately, didn't involve a bridge. It involved certain ceremonies designed to appease some god on the other side, and persuade him to come onto the cliff and help them to find the way across. Of course, his work involved the same errors that everyone else's attempts had: he didn't know what god was on the other side. So, he just came out the morning after the camp noticed that Tony's bridge had totally collapsed, and someone else had fallen, trying to walk on this bridge that could support no one.

So, Karol said, "God of the earth and all good things, I ask that you would come amidst your people, and make known your paths, that your people may enjoy your life and providence." Lucis must have been very happy to hear this, because as soon as Karol had spoken out, he started to speak.

"I, Allahtah, am the god of your people and of the earth. Come, make sacrifices unto me, and walk in my paths, that I may be your god."

Karol took a lamb, slew it, and said to the camp,

"Brethren, pray with me that this sacrifice will be found acceptable to the sight of Allahtah."

"We pray, oh Allahtah, that you would find this sacrifice acceptable from our hands, for our good and the good of all this, your people."

"I, Allahtah, accept your sacrifice as a sign of your allegiance. As my people, you shall start your day with a sacrifice and with a psalm unto me, your god. And you shall rejoice throughout the day, and you shall tell the world, that I Allahtah, have redeemed you. On Sunday, it shall be a holy day unto me, and you shall come into the assembly. Before you come into the assembly, you shall confess your transgressions before the minister, that you may come before me with a clear conscience and be worthy to stand before my presence."

"Today, with the blessings of our god, Allahtah, let us have the assembly required in his proclamation before the people. Any who need to confess, line up behind this tree." Karol indicated a tree near his tent, as he went in.

And the people came by, confessed, and went out. The last person went out of confession, and it was time to start the assembly. Karol walked up to the front of the people who had gathered in the middle of the camp.

"Let us begin the Assembly to honor our god, Allahtah, the holy." Everyone bowed their heads as Karol went through a long liturgy that had been planted in his head the day before. If you were to see the way that Lucis stood laughing in victory, you would be genuinely frightened.

I doubt that any of the poor people could see Lucis standing and laughing, but as the people went on with assembly after assembly, god wasn't doing anything for them. All they could do was to pray for something to happen, but week after week, month after month, year after year, nothing happened. It looked as if Karol wouldn't make it, either. He didn't. Instead, he died.

And, when he woke up, he was in a black robe in some kind of holding cell room. He couldn't tell where he was, why he was there, or how he got there. He only knew that he did not want to be in that room. Suddenly, he began to remember the assemblies he had held during his time down on the earth.

The door opened. "I see you're ready for judgment?" Something said. He started walking with this thing. It led him to a throne on which another thing called Melech Ha-Olam sat. He bowed to Melech Ha-Olam and said, "Hail to thee, Allahtah, my god and my redeemer."

"Whatever," Melech Ha-Olam said. He opened a book and read through it for several hours, after which he opened another book and read it for several more hours.

"Wajitylla, Karol. Idolater. Explains that special greeting you gave me..." And Melech Ha-Olam went on for days, reading everything that Karol has ever done. Afterwards, judgment was passed: "Condemned." Karol walked out a door that opened right in front of him and fell into the canyon. He now spends eternity with his other two friends, Ron and Tony, staring at each and yelling out in pain and sorrow from the lake of fire between the two canyon walls.

Polymorphism

———————————— ◆ ————————————

Unfortunately, I cannot say that no one else fell between the canyon, because there were plenty of other people, who decided to attempt to cross, who, of course, never made it. But, one person had an interesting thing to say about it.

Martin decided to give righteousness another go across the canyon, and he decided to try to build his bridge with an outrageous amount of supports. Sixty years he had worked, building his bridge inch by inch, just like Ron had. But, also like Ron, his righteousness was impure, and became more so as the bridge moved across the canyon. But, while he worked replacing several key supports, he noticed that there was a bridge several miles away that everyone else had missed. He stopped what he was doing and stared hard at it for a while, and then he ran back to the side. He ran out of camp and into the forest to try and find this bridge.

There was a clear path to the bridge, but that had been concealed and was now replaced by such thick vegetation that he would have to examine practically every step he took, which would be impossible by all the vines in the path. It almost looked like he could actually tell where the path used to lie because that's where the vegetation is the thickest now.

And, on the other side of the vegetation, there stands Lucis, guarding the bridge, trying to keep the people from finding it. He instructs the religious leaders to deny its existence (if they even know that it does exist), and he keeps the civil authorities sharp, looking and ready to pounce on any sign of the bridge or any person who knows anything about it. Poor Martin was the victim of a cover-up.

David was staring at the ceiling in his little bedroom in uptown Geyser Springs as he had just waked up. As he lay there, the thoughts of the canyon were ringing through his head. Particularly haunting were King Lucis' words, "You belong to me." David couldn't understand such a statement from this thing that he had never seen before, yet he had the feeling that it was still hanging around somewhere in the room.

Back to the religious people David went, looking for new answers. He was inquiring about a canyon far away that seems to have some unknown bearing on the course of events in his life. He asked. The leaders hardly understood what he was talking about, but one knew. "Well, there is a canyon being crossed that explorers seem to think we need across, but no one has managed to actually cross it."

"What's on the other side?" David asked.

"No one knows. I think we'll never know. Don't worry about it, though. I'm sure you can find your way across."

"How?" David asked.

"No god would actually keep someone from crossing."

"How do you know that? Have you actually met this god?"

"It just stands to reason that he wouldn't keep you out unless you were really bad."

"I had a dream last night."

"We all dream. Don't worry about it."

"I dreamed that some god told me that no one has crossed because no one is worthy to cross."

"Have you killed anyone?"

"No."

"Stolen anything of value from someone or organization?"

"No."

"Ever done anything really bad?"

"I fought with a friend."

"And?"

"I punched him in the nose. It started bleeding and he was unconscious for some time, but he was back up in a very short time."

"Did you mean to do that?"

"No."

"Then you have no problem."

"How would you know?"

"I'm the religious, right? I'm supposed to know these things."

"You just might know a little less than you think you do."

As the two talked in Geyser Springs, someone was preparing to cross the bridge. His name was Sprite, and he was an announcer for Melech Ha-Olam.

Since he had the time, David decided to come to the canyon and see how the explorers were doing. He walked in to see some very rough looking people, some mourning the loss of the late Karol Wajitylla, who was supposed to be able to get Allahtah to bridge the canyon. Most of the camp was in assembly, preparing for the coming of Allahtah, except for Martin, who was trying to find a way to the bridge.

"Hi, I'm David. I'm interested in learning about your work," David said, talking to one of the less rough-looking people.

"Well, we have had some bridges built, but none of the bridges ever supported anyone. Three have been lost while trying to cross. We don't know how to make a useable bridge, so someone found a god to do most of the work for us."

"A god?"

"Yes. Allahtah will take care of the canyon."

A voice was heard from behind a pile of bushes. "Allahtah won't help," it said, "The real bridge is hidden in the bushes."

"What was that?" David asked.

"What was what?" The other guy said.

"Someone spoke from behind the bushes."

"I didn't hear anything."

"Leave camp and follow a path to a very thick patch of bushes. If you can get through, you can find the bridge," the voice said.

"Don't listen to that stupid liar! There is no bridge and never will be. You don't need a bridge." Another voice said. This voice was a very gruff voice that seemed to have been disguised to sound very kind and attractive. David just stood there, thinking. Two people were talking to him from behind the bushes, and he didn't know who was right. There was only one way to find out.

"I think I'm going to walk around for a while," David said, and slowly and reluctantly, moving back and searching for the path that the first voice spoke of.

Martin was still looking through the shrubbery as David walked up.

"Hello, young man. How'd you get here?" He asked. "I just decided to come and see the canyon, and see if it is really as uncross-able as it seems."

"It hasn't been crossed yet, but there's a bridge back there somewhere. I saw it while I was working on my bridge. The only question is, how do I get there?"

"What about Allahtah?"

"A voice from behind the bushes told me that Allahtah won't do anything."

"Why is everyone else waiting for Allahtah's appearance, then?"

"Because another voice behind the bushes tells them that Allahtah is still coming, but that he will take a long time to prepare a bridge."

"Why don't you listen to that one?"

"Because it's gruff. It can't be telling the truth."

"So you tried to find another way."

"I tried to build a bridge with my righteousness, and I noticed that a bridge was already built about a mile from camp. I decided to try to get to that bridge."

"This is the only way there?"

"The bridge is hidden somewhere behind all this vegetation."

"Can't you crawl under the bushes?"

"No. Something won't let me pass."

Jerry Bartolomy was beginning to squeeze the trigger of the family's revolver as a voice came from behind the bushes, "Drop the gun and listen." It was a very kind voice, very concerned about what was happening. Another voice came out from behind the bushes. This voice was a gruff voice disguised to sound kind. It said, "Don't pay any attention. Just pull the trigger. You'll be glad you did." Jerry began to pull harder.

"NO! DON'T! There's another way," the first voice said.

"Sprite doesn't know what he's talking about."

"I do too. Lucis is lying to you. Drop the gun and listen."

"Kill yourself. Don't let Sprite take advantage of you like that. You came here to die, so die."

"There's a better way."

"No, there isn't."

"Look below you." Jerry was suddenly transported to the edge of a very large canyon as Sprite said this. He looked down and, to his horror, he saw a huge lake of fire that covered the entire expanse of the canyon floor. "If you pull that trigger, that's where you'll go," the first voice said.

"No, you won't. It'll be the end of your problems." The second voice said.

"It may be the end of your problems up here, but you'll have more down there." Jerry stared below him again.

"It isn't that bad," the second voice said.

"That's right. It's worse. Worse than you can imagine. Drop the gun and listen." Jerry dropped the gun. "Good. Now, find a little dirt trail. If you follow it, you can find a group of people looking for a bridge. Stay with them." Jerry found the trail, and the people, and stayed out of view as he watched them work.

"I have a feeling that the bridge is the only way across this canyon," Martin said as he turned around to face the two boys standing behind him. "It would certainly explain why we haven't made it across."

"Where is it?" Jerry asked as he stared at the solid collection of shrubbery.

"It's back there. Somewhere."

"How can we get to it?"

"I don't know. It's hard to find. I can't see it. I can't see the path to it. It ends right here." Martin pointed to a dirt path that continued under the shrubbery. "We have to go under the shrubbery."

"Can you?"

"I don't know. Something seems to be blocking me, but I'm not sure what."

"I want out of this miserable place," Jerry said, and he took off under the bushes, crawling and snaking his way faster than Martin, or even David, could go. Eventually, he came to the heaviest and whitest wrought-iron fence that you could imagine possible.

"That explains why I can't get through." Martin said. They watched all the people that they could see in that clearing right in front of the bridge, and saw people who you could tell were not citizens of the Kingdom of Death. Whenever you see a citizen of the Kingdom of Death, you can't really sense much peace or happiness in them. Some of the citizens do smile, but you could tell that the smile is a kind of mask behind which hides stress and nervousness over practically nothing. But all of the people they were looking at were smiling, and not just to hide their emotions from themselves and others. Martin could tell that the smile on every face came from a life of peace and happiness.

Someone saw them looking under the fence and started to come to talk to them, but then hesitated and said, "Follow the bushes to a gate. I'll tell you how to get in. Don't try coming in here, though, because anyone who comes in any other way is a thief and a liar." As he finished saying this, the ugliest man you could ever see started dragging Jerry back to the path by his ear while expressly telling Jerry why he should have killed himself.

"What was that?" David asked as he watched King Lucis taking Jerry out, trying to keep a safe distance from him and stay close to Martin as they crawled back to the path.

"That is the fellow who's been hindering me the whole time. I'll bet he planted this shrubbery here to keep us from seeing that bridge."

"Not so," said King Lucis, as he started to pull the remaining two with Jerry out to the path, "Your ancestors planted those shrubs when they chose to sell their souls to me."

Instantiation

◆

Two millennia ago, someone had crossed the canyon, yet not necessarily the bridge. The bridge that existed at that time was rickety and old, not strong enough to hold many people. This man, Melech Ha Olam's son just came flying right in and snuck over onto man's side without anyone knowing it. Once there, however, in a little stable behind a hotel in Bethlehem, King Lucis had mixed feelings about his being there. Lucis knew that this man's presence would endanger his rule over the Kingdom of Death. He also knew that this man was Melech Ha-Olam's only idea to get a substantial bridge built. So, if he could it could be the end of Melech's ongoing interference with Lucis' plans.

Once he realized this, killing the man became Lucis' top priority. He was obsessed with it. When the man was still a little boy in a stable, he sent soldiers out to kill him. Of course, Melech Ha-Olam warned the boy's parents and they made off to somewhere in Egypt. Then, Nazareth.

The boy was safe for now, but as he kept growing, Sprite would carry instructions from Melech Ha-Olam to the boy. Eventually, the instructions became very threatening to King lucis, so he became very aware that his reign would end shortly if nothing could be done.

Plenty was done about this boy. After he met his friend, John, at the River Jordan, he became known for who he was throughout the entire Kingdom of Death, and he would go about teaching about Melech Ha-

Olam's kingdom. So, he became an easy target for King Lucis. At least it seemed that way.

Some of his teachings could be considered, well, illogical. It is actually possible that he could offend someone. In fact he did, either that or King lucis told some people to be offended. Whatever the case, some people began to get angry with this man, and eventually wanted to kill him. Time after time, someone would come up to him, but somehow, the man could escape death time after time, even escaping a mob that seeked to stone him dead.

But then, he came to a city called Jerusalem, where the luck seemed to stop. After being cheered by all of his supporters as they watched him enter the city, the city seemed to turn against him as the governing body of the whole province of Palestine began to seek to try him falsely. Then, one of his friends cut a deal with one of the court officials: information for thirty silver coins. They struck a deal, and Melech Ha-Olam's son was turned over to the court officials. First, the Judenite Ecclesiastical Court tried him, and they couldn't find any actual witnesses, so someone found willing liars to come up and lie about the man. Then it was off to the official Roman court. That part was easy. All the people had to do was rally. The governor was obviously very reluctant to punish the man, but the people scared him into it. So the man was sent to a cross to die. King Lucis spent the weekend celebrating the end of the Kingdom of Life.

But, something went wrong. Sunday morning, the man was seen out and running about through the streets of some cities surrounding Jerusalem. Then, he flew off to the Kingdom of Life to report the success to Melech Ha-Olam. A brand new bridge was seen spanning the width of Thelto Canyon. King Lucis knew that this could mean trouble, so he built a wall to keep the people in the Kingdom of Darkness trapped, and then he planted some pretty shrubbery to hide the wall.

Compiler

◆

David and Martin were following a long path of shrubbery trying to find Jerry, who had run off along the path the moment he was out of the bushes. As they walked along the lush green forest that surrounded them, they saw him standing in front of a large wooden capital 't.' On the capital 't' were the words, "Kingdom of Death keep out. This land and bridge are claimed by His Mercifulness, Melech Ha-Olam, ruler of the Kingdom of Life. Citizens only beyond this point." Poor Jerry was standing right beside that sign, watching all the people inside move about inside the compound and cross the bridge freely. He earnestly wished he could just tear down the cross that held him outside and force his way in.

David and Martin caught up to Jerry and stood behind him, waiting for the man who had spoken to them. What came up to them was a little different than they expected. King Lucis came up to them face-to-face and said, "Stop this treason!" He started to walk forward and the poor threesome were forced to simply walk backward to keep from being run over by this hideous monster that was charging them. The man they were waiting for suddenly came up to King Lucis and shouted directly at him, "Shut up, slime bag!" Lucis simply turned and tried to attack his antagonist, but before he could reach him, Sprite came out and delivered such a swat on poor Lucis' head that it sent the Death-King running for his life.

"Okay, so, I'm Kevin Bailey. Pleased to meet ya'll." The other guy said. "Ya'll want to know how to get in, right?"

"We want to see how to cross the canyon." Martin said, as he had taken upon himself to speak for the group.

"That bridge behind me is the only way to get across. I don't know what ya'll have been trying to do, but any bridge made by ya'll will never do."

"Can you make a bridge?"

"'Fraid not. That bridge leads to the Kingdom of Life. If you expect to make it across, you have to belong on that side. We do. Ya'll don't. That's why this large Cross can keep you out. You don't belong."

"But we've made some bridges."

"Try to approach someone for the sole purpose of hating that person, and then make a lasting relationship with that person. Can you?"

"No."

"That's a problem. Everyone on this side of the Cross-and across the canyon-is a friend of His Mercifulness, Melech Ha-Olam. If you don't know him personally, you've no chance to even come into our little cove, let alone onto the shores of the Kingdom of Life. There's no way. Your bridges turn into pure unworthiness as they come across. Do you know that? We can never make a bridge because all our righteousness and our good works turns into pure unworthiness, evil, and unrighteousness by the time you get across the canyon. Think any king will let someone into his kingdom who can only reap destruction and end up claiming it for the kingdom of Death? Because that's what you'd have to do—start a little war. It's too late. The war's started, and my king has a defense around his Kingdom. Your king can't do anything about us. Think my king will let ya'll in? You have to come through the Cross. Otherwise, you're nothing but thieves and liars. And thieves and liars don't get across the canyon. They end up down in the lake of fire that burns forever right smack dab in the middle of this here canyon."

"How'd you get over here?"

"That's the funny thing. You see, all of us over on this side of the Cross are your people regenerate."

"What?"

"We defected."

"We want to defect. Let us in."

"That's not how it works. You have to go through the cross."

"What?"

"Judas Iscariot."

"What?"

"Judas Iscariot. He tried to pretend to be one of us, but then he betrayed us and sent my king's son to his death."

"So?"

"He pretended to defect."

"So?"

"Melech Ha-Olam isn't going to let that happen again. Anyone who comes in here must defect not only in action and in thought, but also in his heart. In fact, the defection must be made in your heart before you can come in here."

"What?"

"In other words," Jerry said as he turned his head to look at the two behind him, "you are naturally disloyal as you are."

"How does he know that?" Martin asked, his face beginning to glow with rage.

"Because of the Judas man," David said. "Okay, Kev, tell us what to do."

"Do you realize that you've been disloyal to the Kingdom of Life?"

"This is stupid!" Martin said. "I'm going to get back to work on my bridge."

"I wouldn't do that, sir." Kevin said while walking by the Cross and coming to him.

"Defecting again, are you?"

"No, sir. I do this all the time. You see, I come into your kingdom to lead defectors across this here boundary." Kevin indicated the cross.

"See you kids on the other side and shut up, stupid." Martin raced back to camp and got back to work on his bridge, moving sections around until it seemed to begin to become a copy of the one that spans the canyon already.

"I'll have to pray for him," Kevin said. "Wait for me." He rushed back across the Cross and to the people who stood inside and spoke very quickly with one. As he turned to come back to the two still waiting for him, the one he spoke with took another person by the hand and together they rushed across the canyon.

"Where are they going?" David asked.

"They're going to entreat Melech Ha-Olam about your other friend, to see if he can still be rescued"

"Anyway, what do I need to do?"

"You realize that you are disloyal to the Kingdom of Life and to its precepts, right?"

"I have had no reason to keep them."

"My king has power over your kingdom. He still judges all of you. His rules apply even on this side of the canyon. Do you realize that you have been disloyal to them?"

"Yes."

"And you?" Kevin stared at Jerry.

"Uhh, yeah." Jerry said and let his head drop down over his shoulders.

"Do you know what the penalty for that is?"

"What!?" Both of the two defection candidates looked up at Kevin in a very shocked surprise.

"As I said, my King has authority in even your kingdom. That includes the authority to judge every one over here for disloyalty. After all, King Lucis is actually a disloyal subject of Melech Ha-Olam."

"That isn't very fair," Jerry said as he stared at Kevin.

"That's why he sends people in to give you a chance to defect."

"Oh."

"So, do you know what the penalty for disloyalty is?"

"No, what?"

"Death."

"He kills us just because we don't know any better?"

"Ya'll do know better. Most people have a sense of belonging to some other kingdom. And, we have speakers running around."

"But it doesn't work for some."

"Anyone who wants to defect can."

"How?"

"Because Melech Ha-Olam will send someone to meet up with defectors at the right time. That could even be how ya'll got here."

"But what about the others?"

"If someone doesn't want something, why offer?"

"So that they know that it's there?"

"There are certain people who won't want this opportunity even if it hits them in the face three-thousands times during their life. Melech Ha-Olam knows who they are, and he makes sure that people who have a desire get a speaker, and sometimes it means that less desiring people have to go without, but some of those would probably not defect, or if one does, then he or she would be more likely to just put defection on hold and try to conform back to living like the regular old citizen of the Kingdom of Death, which would be kind of bad in itself. Anyway, Melech Ha-Olam knows who those people are, and he can get the speakers to people who need them, who desire defection, because that's the way to really make the kingdom of life grow. Let wanters in, and let those wanters bring in the others."

"What about wanters who don't get to hear from a speaker?"

"Anyone who wants it will."

"Okay, go on."

"Right. The penalty is death, and then there's the bridge."

"That's important?"

"Yes."

"How."

"Because of the way it was built. You see, this canyon wasn't always here."

"You mean, the Kingdom of Death was…"

"The Kingdom of Death didn't always exist. It was the product of a rebellion led by King Lucis. The whole world used to be under the complete dominion of the Kingdom of Life."

"What happened?"

"king Lucis used to be a high ranking official in the Kingdom of Life, but he decided that he could be a better king than Melech Ha-Olam. He became very proud of this opinion of his, and began to get a gathering of subjects for a revolution."

"And he won?"

"No. Actually, he was exiled. The only reason that the Kingdom of Death is here is because he snuck back into the Kingdom of Life to try to recruit your Ancestors."

"My Ancestors fought him off, right?"

"No. Actually, they were deceived into going right off to war. They defected, and the Thelto Canyon split in order to protect melech Ha-Olam's kingdom."

"From what?"

"Further interference. He isn't ready to allow King Lucis back into his realm."

"So, can I defect?"

"You need to know a little bit before you do."

"Right. Go on."

"Of all his subjects, your ancestors were the closest to Melech Ha-Olam. In fact, of all that he created, your ancestors were the only ones that were made by hand. Everything else was just spoken into existence. We were formed, built, and then breathed into."

"Breathed into?"

"The Life-Breath. That's the thing that tells you that you don't belong in the Kingdom of Death. It's the Life Breath that keeps your people so interested in religion, and it's still that same Life-Breath that makes some of the people in the Kingdom of Death defect."

"So what, am I supposed to be rescued by that?"

"No. It is actually something that all the citizens in the Kingdom of Death lack. It's what actually makes the Kingdom of Death such a bad place to be.

"So, how could this Life-Breath push people to defection?"

"It's something that everyone is meant to have—built to have-needs to have. If you don't, you can feel it. You can see it, even."

"How?"

"I'm sure you've noticed that most of the people in the Kingdom of Death don't actually feel any peace, right? Some will even drug themselves to death just to feel a little bit of peace. What they're actually trying to do is to use a chemical substitute for the life-Breath."

"Will it work?"

"It seems to at first, but then it wears off. It could work if the Life-Breath is a chemical, but it isn't. It's actually a force that works to sustain the human spirit."

"So, if I don't have this breath, my spirit is dead, right?"

"No. But it does mean that you will experience something much worse than death"

"That's crazy. I'd be dead, too, wouldn't I?"

"Not necessarily. But it does mean that you can never experience any kind of happiness, peace, or serenity."

"Neither can ya'll, right?"

"Every one of us does, actually."

"How?"

"Remember what I told you the penalty for being disloyal to the Kingdom of life and its precepts are?"

"Death."

"Works two ways. There are actually two deaths, one which every one of us, you and me will have to experience, a physical death. And then, there's a much worse spiritual death that your people go through."

"What's so bad about the spiritual death? It's just eternal nonexistence, right?"

"No. You know that lake of fire at the bottom of the canyon?"

"Yeah?"

"That's the spiritual death. You get to be tossed into that lake of fire, and you stay down there forever."

"That's cruel."

"It's fair."

"How?"

"Because you are disloyal to the Kingdom of Life. The penalty of disloyalty is death."

"So, your telling me that I'm hopelessly doomed to eternal hellfire?"

"As you are, yes. In reality? No."

"What?"

"If you don't do anything about it, you are. However, there is something you can do. Or, rather, something that has been done about it."

"What?"

"Melech Ha-Olam's son died down here."

"So?"

"He managed to remain totally innocent down here, so he never really belonged to your kingdom. King Lucis tried to keep him from accomplishing his mission, but there was one thing he didn't know. The son's mission was to be killed."

"Why would that help me?"

"Because Melech Ha-Olam was able to transfer the guilt of every single person to his son. That way, defection would be possible."

"So every person is found innocent?"

"No. Every person can be made innocent. Melech Ha-Olam allows every person to choose between kingdoms. If you want to remain in the Kingdom of Death, you can. If you want to defect, you can too. The only thing is, if you remain in your kingdom, you will have to face the consequences."

"I can see how that's fair."

"But, you have the opportunity to defect. That's what the Son bought for us. An opportunity. It's a question of which side of the Cross you want to be on."

"The Cross?"

"Yes, the Cross. This thing here that guards the gates. You can never enter without going through the Cross."

"Why?"

"Melech Ha-Olam's son died on one."

"Why does that matter?"

"Because it's that very same Cross that divides my people from yours."

"I see. How exactly can you get to the other side?"

"Because the Cross is emblazoned on my spirit as a mark of ownership. Plus, the life-breath is restored in me."

"So, how does this Cross get emblazoned on your spirit?"

"I defected. It's what happens when someone defects. You get it to identify you as a part of the Kingdom."

"I think I'd like to defect now. Do I just walk across the Cross?"

"If you try to, you'd look like an intruder. You can't get across the Cross until you are a citizen of the Kingdom of Life, and you can't become a citizen by just willing it or accepting that it exists. You have to declare your defection."

"I have to what?"

"Declare defection. You have to tell Melech Ha-Olam that you plan to defect."

"But he's on the other side of the canyon."

"He can hear a defector's declaration."

"From across the canyon?"

"He can't hear normal prayer prayers from your people, but a declaration of defection he will hear."

"How do I do it?"

"It's rather simple, actually. Do you believe that you have been disloyal?"

"Yes."

"Do you believe that his son died for you?"

"Does that matter?"

"Yes, because someone has to be punished for your wrongdoing, and it could be either you or a perfectly innocent person."

"Oh. Melech Ha-Olam's son was"

"Perfectly innocent."

"Okay, I believe it."

"Are you willing to turn from disloyalty?"

"I guess."

"Are you sorry that you were disloyal?"

"What's it to you?"

"Because part of defecting is an apology for past disloyalty and becoming loyal to a new king."

"Same question."

"Think you can serve two kings? Its awfully hard, and you'll most likely end up back in the service of King Lucis. You have to give that up to defect."

"Okay. I do."

"Good. Is Melech Ha-Olam your Lord?"

"He will be."

"You not only need to become disloyal to Lucis, you must announce a new lordship. Is Melech Ha-Olam your lord?"

"I guess."

"Good. Now, what you need to do is to tell Melech Ha-Olam everything that you just told me."

David and Jerry started to talk to each other, giving each other inquisitive faces and wondering how to make this statement as Sprite walked right up to face them and said, "Go ahead." They did, and Sprite was off running across the bridge.

Exception

◆

Martin was back to his bridge repairs, but then he looked over to the other side of Thelto Canyon, and he saw that there was a smaller distance between his side and the other if he could get closer to the bridge. He started moving. First came the total dismantling of his bridge, which he carried, piece by piece, to another spot, a little ridge jutting out in front of a group of very rich and thick shrubbery. Had he looked closer, he would have seen that the shrubbery hides a wrought-iron fence.

Daniel was getting a little desperate for a visit with the pastor of First Baptist Church of Geyser Springs, Co, as he left the school early Monday afternoon. Someone had recently announced the untimely deaths of two of the school's main druggies, and the expulsion of three others. Daniel had become interested in John's church, First Baptist, as he saw David and Jerry being thrown across the hall by the school's most prominent football player. They simply walked back to their spots, Jerry holding his broken jaw.

John had been taken by surprise when Daniel showed up for church the Sunday before, but he was somewhat glad, since he had company in case he couldn't take the nap he was planning to take. He awoke to see the pastor's eyes focused straight on him, the statement coming out of his mouth, "The wages of sin is death." Daniel looked at him and said, "What's sin?"

"I have no idea. I think it's some thing you do, but I'm not sure what. If someone tries to talk to me about it, I just pretend that I'm uncomfortable with the idea. It keeps the pastor away, and that's how I suggest you react to him when he starts talking to you about it." John said.

"I think I'd rather like to hear him out. I'm curious."

"You'll be sorry."

"How do you know?"

"I know, Daniel. I've fell victim to nearly everybody's efforts to convert me. You won't like it. They don't make sense, and they don't leave you alone."

"You just don't listen."

"Yeah, well, I've been around these guys. I know the message. I may not know the terms, but I can give you the message without the hassle."

"Okay, shoot. Never mind."

After another song was sung, it was time to leave. John started to explain the 'message' to Daniel. "Where do you want me to start," he asked.

"At the beginning."

"There are so many."

"Sin would be a good start."

"Okay, sin is something bad. I know it's something you do, but I'm not sure what. But basically, these people teach that you are doomed to fiery Hell until you repent and are either born again or saved or something."

"Which one?"

"Whichever you prefer."

After that conversation, Daniel would started to pace about more often at school, and when the school announced the deaths of the two druggies, Daniel had a little revelation. He realized that the preacher must have been talking about death coming from extremely bad behavior.

Martin started to build his bridge as he looked over and saw that he could get an even shorter gap. He started to gather the myriad of braces and supports that he had to carry with him and took them to a ridge that jutted out even further than the one he stood on. He looked over and found that he was about five yards from the other bridge, and the shrubbery was so large and close, and the ridge was so thin that he was forced to bend over and look straight down into the canyon and the lake of fire as he started to prepare to put his first brace in place.

John came up to Daniel at their spot at the lockers Tuesday morning. They both looked across the hall, were David and Jerry stood and Puntz, the quarterback, was about to walk by again. Daniel's face was red, but he seemed to be a little calmer.

"How do you plan to get into Heaven?" He asked as the pacing started up again.

"Don't worry about it," John said in the most reassuring voice he could muster, "us good guys don't have a problem. We'll make it."

"How, though."

"We can find out when we get there."

Martin looked over to the white bridge just five yards away and saw that he could get an even shorter gap. He started tearing down the braces and dragging them closer. He stopped after about a yard and put one of the braces down. He had to use his free hand to hold himself up on the tree branches that hung over the canyon; he was practically climbing trees now, because he could find very little ground. As he worked, a voice from behind the trees said, "Whoever enters in by any other way is a thief and a liar. Go around and find the Cross, it's the only way in."

Puntz came back up to David and Jerry as they stood in their customary spot, and Daniel, much to John's disappointment, was watching again. BAANNG, they hit the wall again, and Daniel was *really* pacing now. He was moving so fast that his rubber soles should have melted the tile floor.

"John, how do you know you're right?" He asked. John simply stared straight through Daniel, watching him change his pace several times; taking every corner sharp and fast enough to make most of us topple over.

"Simple. I don't let those two freak me out." John let his face turn into an assorted rainbow of colors as he watched Daniel start up again. "You know, I think you would be over whatever it is by now."

"Why?"

"I've seen the same things you have, and you don't see me walking 'round, do you?"

"I just can't help it."

"Sure you can." Daniel walked right up to John.

"John, I've been thinking about you're church thing."

"You got a way out?"

"No. I'm confused. You say you have no desire to be there?"

"It's a good time to catch up on sleep, but that's all it's really good for."

"Yet, you say that you have and know what those two have?" Daniel pointed to David as a piece of paper changed hands.

"I believe so."

"How?"

"I go to their church, don't I?"

"But not willingly. You don't even pretend to want to pretend to be there. Don't you think that God knows the difference?"

"Why would he care?"

"Hypocrisy."

"What?"

"I'm sure you've heard the phrase, 'you get what you give?' well, what you give is letting everyone know that church is the absolute last place you want to be. Wouldn't it logically follow, then, that you would get God letting the whole church know that you are the last person he wants to do anything for?"

"I thought that God is loving."

"Think about it. You're expecting him to be a slave."

"So?"

"The whole thought of a sovereign being is negated by that type of thinking. You don't really believe, man."

"So?" John let his face, which was beginning to return to its normal color, turn a very fiery red.

Martin saw that he could build his bridge in an even smaller gap, about an inch from the bridge, so he started moving and one by one put the pieces together, sometimes trying to hold onto the bridge for support, but then he noticed that the bridge beside would not support him. He didn't think anything of it as he started building his intricate series of braces and brace-braces into the canyon wall, and then started to build the bridge right across the canyon, only…snap! Something broke. Martin reached up to grab onto the real bridge, but his hand went straight through, and he fell into the Lake of Fire.

The next Sunday, Daniel came to church again, and John was dragged in following, but he perked up as soon as he saw Daniel. He fought out of his parents' grip and ran up to meet his friend. But something odd happened just as he was running down the sanctuary: everyone disappeared. John looked around to see piles of clothing, but other than that no trace of anyone of the people who only seconds before were sitting in the almost packed sanctuary. Now, no one was to be found anywhere in the church except John and Daniel.

"My parents!" John shouted. "Were did they go?"

"John, this is exactly what I was telling you several days ago. I heard the sermon yesterday, and you apparently didn't. The whole church went to heaven."

"You mean that the whole church just died? Where are the corpses?"

"No, John. The preacher preached on some occurrence in which the Christians are taken into heaven."

"Ah, yes, the rapture. Daniel, I want to point something out to you."

"What?"

"*Every* Christian was supposed to disappear."

"So?"

"You consider yourself Christian, right?"

"Yes."

"Why are you still here?"

Seven years after that fateful day, John and Daniel woke up in a holding cell. After sometime, Melech Ha-Olam came up to them and unlocked the cell. They were lead up to some place that they couldn't describe, except for a great white throne. As they looked around them, they noticed that the whole earth seemed to be running away, and then heaven, and right below them, the lake of fire opened up. They looked back at the white throne, where judgment was passed: "Condemned."

0-595-22957-3

www.ingramcontent.com/pod-product-compliance
Lightning Source LLC
Chambersburg PA
CBHW051254050326
40689CB00007B/1195